Blackbeard the Pirate

First published in 2006 by
Franklin Watts
338 Euston Road
London
NW1 3BH

Franklin Watts Australia
Level 17/207 Kent Street
Sydney
NSW 2000

A CIP catalogue record for this book is available from the British Library.

ISBN 978 0 7496 6690 3

Series Editor: Jackie Hamley
Series Advisor: Dr Barrie Wade
Series Designer: Peter Scoulding

Printed in China

Franklin Watts is a division of
Hachette Children's Books,
an Hachette Livre UK company.

Blackbeard the Pirate

by Mick Gowar and Mike Phillips

FRANKLIN WATTS
LONDON • SYDNEY

My name is John. When I was a small boy I fought the fiercest pirate in the world! This is my story.

It was a hot summer day. I was fishing for crabs in the harbour of Sark island. I looked out to sea.

A ship was in the distance. It had black sails and a black flag with white bones and a skull. Pirates!

The pirates rowed ashore.
Their captain had burning fuses
in his hair. He looked like a devil!
"My name is Blackbeard,"
he shouted. "I am the lord
of this island now."

The pirates forced all the people to bring their money and jewels to the churchyard.

Blackbeard took everything and
locked everyone in the church.

But I was so small that nobody noticed me. No one saw me climb into my little boat and sail away.

I sailed to the next island. There was a warship in the harbour.

"There are pirates on the Isle of Sark," I told the Captain.
"Please help us."
"How?" asked the Captain.
"I have a plan," I said.

Next day we sailed into Sark harbour. The Captain and I rowed ashore.

Blackbeard met us. “I am the lord of Sark,” he said. “What do you want?”

"This boy's father was a passenger on my ship," the Captain said. "He died. May we come ashore to bury him?"

"Yes," said Blackbeard, looking at the fine warship he hoped to steal. "But first, you must give me all your guns and swords."

Some of the Captain's sailors rowed ashore with a coffin. Slowly we climbed the hill to the church.

All the people of Sark were inside.

We closed the church doors.

The Captain opened the coffin –
it was filled with guns and swords.

"Now we'll get those pirates,"
said the Mayor. "Follow me!"

Some of the pirates tried to steal the warship. But the Captain had set a trap.

The Mayor and the islanders captured the other pirates and locked them in the church.

"I'll take these pirates to London," said the Captain. "They will be put in prison."

No one saw Blackbeard climb into my little boat and sail away – except me. And no one noticed me because I was so small.

Now I am old, but I still look out to sea every morning and evening to make sure no ship with black sails and a black flag is sailing into the harbour.

Hopscotch has been specially designed to fit the requirements of the National Literacy Strategy. It offers real books by top authors and illustrators for children developing their reading skills. There are 49 Hopscotch stories to choose from:

Marvin, the Blue Pig
ISBN 978 0 7496 4619 6

Plip and Plop
ISBN 978 0 7496 4620 2

The Queen's Dragon
ISBN 978 0 7496 4618 9

Flora McQuack
ISBN 978 0 7496 4621 9

Willie the Whale
ISBN 978 0 7496 4623 3

Naughty Nancy
ISBN 978 0 7496 4622 6

Run!
ISBN 978 0 7496 4705 6

The Playground Snake
ISBN 978 0 7496 4706 3

"Sausages!"
ISBN 978 0 7496 4707 0

Bear in Town
ISBN 978 0 7496 5875 5

Pippin's Big Jump
ISBN 978 0 7496 4710 0

Whose Birthday Is It?
ISBN 978 0 7496 4709 4

The Princess and the Frog
ISBN 978 0 7496 5129 9

Flynn Flies High
ISBN 978 0 7496 5130 5

Clever Cat
ISBN 978 0 7496 5131 2

Moo!
ISBN 978 0 7496 5332 3

Izzie's Idea
ISBN 978 0 7496 5334 7

Roly-poly Rice Ball
ISBN 978 0 7496 5333 0

I Can't Stand It!
ISBN 978 0 7496 5765 9

Cockerel's Big Egg
ISBN 978 0 7496 5767 3

How to Teach a Dragon Manners
ISBN 978 0 7496 5873 1

The Truth about those Billy Goats
ISBN 978 0 7496 5766 6

Marlowe's Mum and the Tree House
ISBN 978 0 7496 5874 8

The Truth about Hansel and Gretel
ISBN 978 0 7496 4708 7

The Best Den Ever
ISBN 978 0 7496 5876 2

ADVENTURE STORIES

Aladdin and the Lamp
ISBN 978 0 7496 6692 7

Blackbeard the Pirate
ISBN 978 0 7496 6690 3

George and the Dragon
ISBN 978 0 7496 6691 0

Jack the Giant-Killer
ISBN 978 0 7496 6693 4

TALES OF KING ARTHUR

1. The Sword in the Stone
ISBN 978 0 7496 6694 1

2. Arthur the King
ISBN 978 0 7496 6695 8

3. The Round Table
ISBN 978 0 7496 6697 2

4. Sir Lancelot and the Ice Castle
ISBN 978 0 7496 6698 9

TALES OF ROBIN HOOD

Robin and the Knight
ISBN 978 0 7496 6699 6

Robin and the Monk
ISBN 978 0 7496 6700 9

Robin and the Silver Arrow
ISBN 978 0 7496 6703 0

Robin and the Friar
ISBN 978 0 7496 6702 3

FAIRY TALES

The Emperor's New Clothes
ISBN 978 0 7496 7421 2

Cinderella
ISBN 978 0 7496 7417 5

Snow White
ISBN 978 0 7496 7418 2

Jack and the Beanstalk
ISBN 978 0 7496 7422 9

The Three Billy Goats Gruff
ISBN 978 0 7496 7420 5

The Pied Piper of Hamelin
ISBN 978 0 7496 7419 9

HISTORIES

Toby and the Great Fire of London
ISBN 978 0 7496 7079 5 *
ISBN 978 0 7496 7410 6

Pocahontas the Peacemaker
ISBN 978 0 7496 7080 1 *
ISBN 978 0 7496 7411 3

Grandma's Seaside Bloomers
ISBN 978 0 7496 7081 8 *
ISBN 978 0 7496 7412 0

Hoorah for Mary Seacole
ISBN 978 0 7496 7082 5 *
ISBN 978 0 7496 7413 7

Remember the 5th of November
ISBN 978 0 7496 7083 2 *
ISBN 978 0 7496 7414 4

Tutankhamun and the Golden Chariot
ISBN 978 0 7496 7084 9 *
ISBN 978 0 7496 7415 1

*** hardback**